His PERFECT MARTINI

The Cocktail Girls

ANGEL DEVLIN

CONTENTS

The Perfect Martini

Ingredients

1.5 ounces gin
.75 ounce dry vermouth
.75 ounce sweet vermouth
Garnish: olives or lemon twist

Method

Pour into a cocktail mixing glass over ice.
Stir well for 30 seconds
Strain into a chilled cocktail glass
Garnish

Serving suggestion: Pour slowly over various parts of
a hot body and lick off for the best experience.

CHAPTER

One

DAILY NEWS - A British Tabloid
Friday 23 March 2018

HOW FAR IS TOO FAR?
Report by Deanna Murphy

They're worshipped like elite celebrities, but what are the actual talents of the current batch of YouTubers?

Despite a University education resulting in a First Class honours degree in Accountancy, Damien Allen is better known as the brother that plays continual pranks on his elder sister online, including throwing out all of her knickers and replacing them with large granny pants, and placing a fake plastic spider in her lunch.

Another YouTuber, Louis Clayton, amuses his

followers for hours by buying a different car every week and performing drifts in his local supermarket car park when it's closed on a Sunday. He also uploads several 'hilarious' videos of him in supermarkets changing lettered mugs around to spell rude words.

Despite this, these men are becoming worth hundreds of thousands of pounds through sponsorships. Both began by filming themselves playing online games but migrated to the more lucrative 'reality' style uploads.

Chatting to parents online, most despair at their offspring watching these videos of grown men acting like teenagers and leading their kids astray.

Donna Lowe, 28, from Southampton, stated, "I got a phone call from my local supermarket that my son had had his scooter taken off him due to health and safety concerns. He had been performing stunt tricks in the aisles while recording himself, having seen Louis do it the week before. The fact is this guy is only a few years younger than I am. He should try to be a more positive role model for the kids."

CHAPTER Two

YouTube vlog - Uploaded by Louis Clayton on Thurs 22 April 2018

"Hey there, subscribers. So thanks for tuning in. In today's video we're off to McDonald's to buy three hundred boxes of fries to see what we win in the latest Monopoly promotion. It's gonna be a blast. I've got Jonno here with me, Max is coming, and Cam. It's gonna be amazing. I can't wait to see their faces when we rock up to the drive thru and ask for three hundred fries. Let's go."

Louis

Saturday 24 April 2018

I sat back on my large leather corner sofa in my five-bedroomed detached home in Leeds. My YouTube video played on the 60-inch television screen in front of me while I listened on surround sound. I was famous in Britain—well getting there—for doing stuff like this... buying fucking fries.

A computer game nerd, I'd started recording myself playing games like Call of Duty and GTA, getting a following and making a name for myself. Then the sponsorships started coming in and I needed to release more videos. People wanted to get to know me. They felt they did know me. So next it was pranks. I'd prank my friends. Before I knew it, I'd got merch deals. There was the foulest smelling aftershave with my name on it, it was like frikking fly spray.

Now at twenty-five years old I'd just got 750,000 views of me buying fries. For fuck's sake. The money was amazing. The fact I made a living of filming myself was incredible, but again—fucking fries. And it took ages to peel the stickers off the bastards, not to mention the food waste. My mother rang me and had a fit going on about starving children.

I checked my stats. I was at 980,000 subscribers. 20k more and I would have a million—a million. Not views, I quite often got a million and upwards views,

4

but a million people who wanted to see every one of my videos and receive notifications when a new one was uploaded.

I turned to Jonno who was sitting in the leather recliner staring at his iPhone, his hand occasionally dipping into the large packet of crisps on his knee-or potato chips as my US fans called them. I had just started to break the US market. They were my ticket to my first million subscribers, I knew it.

I threw a cushion at Jonno.

"Mate. I need to do something more grown up, get an older audience. I can't keep buying fries."

Jonno shrugged his shoulders at me. "We only won more bloody fries anyway."

"You read that press piece too. They're crucifying me now for the shit kids do. I'm gonna get sued by supermarkets next for crushed tins of beans. I need to move on, get older subscribers, bro."

"So think of something different." He continued to stuff crisps in his mouth.

"What can I do though? I need something elaborate to take me over my first million subscribers. It's got to be epic and appeal to the adult population."

Jonno put his phone down. You have no idea how rare that was to get his full attention.

"Like, streak naked across a football pitch epic?"

I shook my head. "Something totally lit. Bigger. Crazy stupid. Bro, help me think of something."

"In the UK?" He scratched his balls over the top of his joggers.

I sucked on my bottom lip. "Hmmmm... No. Let's go to America. I want to get new fans there. I'll pay for all four of us to go, or the sponsors will. Where shall we go to? New York? Florida?"

"We could do something in Disney World?"

I shook my head. "Nah, I want something more grown up."

"Got it!" Jonno sat up straight. "Let's go to Vegas. There must be a prank we can pull off there. Plus we can hit all the casinos. I've always wanted to go there."

I thought about it. Vegas. I could do a video about gambling a load of money! Hmmm. That was okay, but it wasn't the most exciting thing ever. I mean everyone who went to Vegas did that.

"Hey, we should watch all the movies we can that have Vegas in them, get us in the mood, and get us some ideas." Jonno began scrolling through his phone.

"*Now You See Me*. That's set there. *What*

Happens in Vegas. Nah, that's a chick flick. It's got Ashton Kutcher in it though."

That guy was a legend to us, having been in Punk'd.

"What's it about?" I asked him.

"Man and woman get married in Vegas and have to stay married for a bit. Sounds-"

"Fantastic." I interrupted.

Jonno screwed his face up. "What are you on about, fantastic? You grown a pussy while you're sat there?"

I sit on the very edge of my seat like I'm about to jump up. "No. I mean that's it. I'm gonna Vegas and I'm going to marry a chick there. Some random stranger. Well that'll be my aim anyway. Go to Vegas and see if we can get some chick to marry me. They have to not know who I am though, otherwise I'll get a weird stalker who'll refuse to have an annulment."

"That's the craziest shit I ever heard, man." Jonno said. "You can't do that."

I bounced up out of my chair full of excitement.

"It's epic. It's the most lit idea ever. Let's get on it. Get the others here. We need to plan a holiday."

"You know how your mother reacted to the fries, she's gonna have your balls for this one." Jonno shook his head.

CHAPTER Three

Mila

March 31, 2018 - Saturday

The *Little Black Dress* bar was packed to the hilt. I stood behind the counter with the rest of the evening's crew. My dress was a very short, black lace dress with a nude underlay. It had a steam-punk effect lace design and a scalloped 'v' shape neckline. One of the best parts of working here was being able to dress up, and although we all had to wear black dresses, every one of the cocktail waitresses had their own style.

My dark brown hair was up off my neck in a ponytail and I wore Gucci interlocking stud earrings and a wolf head pendant necklace. They were nice pieces that I had earned and bought myself, something very important to me.

"Can I have a slow comfortable screw... and what cocktails do you do?" The idiot in front of me guffawed at his own joke and then looked at his friends for further encouragement. They never realized I heard this a dozen times a night. Game face on, I gave him my best flirtatious smile.

"You're so amusing." I handed him the cocktail menu. "Now you take a look at that list and see what I can get you. I highly recommend the martini."

The martini was my favorite drink to make. Simple, tasteful, and I made what was called the Perfect Martini with equal amounts of sweet and dry vermouth.

"We want Tequila Slammers." Jerk-off said.

I had to try really hard not to roll my eyes. I added two parts Tequila to six glasses, added the fizz, and placed napkins over the top, placing them on the counter. Jerk-off and his five friends slammed them on the counter, liquid going everywhere before draining what remained in their glasses. "Again." He said, and I fixed them a second lot.

It was typical Vegas. Abandonment of common sense. In here we saw everything. Totally wasted men and women who went on to spend their evenings trying to win a fortune in the casinos. Then there were the couples who had come here to get married. They'd prop up the bar telling me their love stories, with no idea that they were talking to the woman with the most cynical feelings about love. But my game face would be on and I'd sell them champagne cocktails to celebrate the occasion.

And then there were the chumps who came here and got married while they were drunk. They'd hit the bar showing off their wedding rings, and we'd all know that they'd wake up tomorrow with a head full of pain and regret while they found out how to get an annulment post haste.

"Loving the dress tonight." I turned to smile at the owner of the bar, Maximo. A middle-aged sleazeball with a receding hairline and a pot belly, I was sure he thought himself to be some kind of Hugh Hefner. But I liked my job and wanted to keep it, so while ever it was just his eyes on me and not his hands, I'd keep him sweet.

"Thanks. It's a good night tonight." I commented.

"Yeah, takings are up. So I'm a very happy man." He wandered off to mingle with the crowds. In the bar based at the Millennium hotel, Maximo was treated like a celebrity and he ate it up. He probably ate up some of the females who flocked around him attracted to his bank balance too, but that was a visual no one needed in their head, so I went back to work.

During my break I took out my cell from my purse and checked my messages. I had a text from my friend Jenny.

Jenny: I can't wait for tomorrow night. It's going to get wild, girl!

I sighed. I'd been putting her off for weeks and in the end I'd given up. Jenny thought I was quiet, worked too hard, and had decided I needed to see and experience Vegas for myself. She knew I'd come to Vegas following a boyfriend and said it was time to get myself back out there.

My shift over at 2am, I headed back to Spring Valley and hit the sack.

Later that day I woke on the couch, my neck hurting

from the stupid position I'd fallen asleep in. I'd been reading and when my eyes had started to close I'd allowed the tiredness to consume me, placing my eReader on the floor and curling my knees closer to my chest. I checked out the time—9pm—crap!

Swinging my legs off the couch, I sat up, placing my head in my hands, then rubbing at my eyes as I tried to get myself moving. I was meeting Jenny on the Strip at 10:30 pm.

I groaned. Everyone who knew me thought I was a quiet little mouse who needed to experience life. What they didn't understand was I was a quiet little mouse because I'd experienced enough life to last me a lifetime.

I'd arrived in Vegas two years ago at 21, following the 'love of my life'. Against all my family's warnings, I'd followed Billy Hastings to Vegas where we'd hit the Strip and gambled away my savings and allowance before my family had finally had enough of me and cut me off—at which point Billy dumped me.

There was no way I was crawling back to the Upper East Side with my tail between my legs. I'd hated my life there anyway. An endless itinerary of charity functions, dinner events, and parental matchmaking with their idea of suitable future husband material. A return to that, along with constant reminders of how foolish I'd been? Plus what they'd done after my relationship ended... well it was unforgivable. So, no thanks. Instead I'd rented a one bedroom apartment in Spring Valley and got myself a job in a bar.

Tonight, Jenny would expect me to get wasted. The problem was me and alcohol were a heady mix. It didn't take much to get me drunk and when I did, I tended to think stupid things were a great idea, which was why I had a tattoo of a martini cocktail on my right ass cheek. I told you I liked them. One night I'd liked them a little too much...

Dragging myself into the kitchen I started to fix myself an omelet, figuring if I lined my stomach well, the alcohol wouldn't hit as hard.

Stomach full, I dressed in a white tea dress with a lace insert at the waist, and slipped my feet into some white Jimmy Choos, one nod I still had to my previous existence as a rich bitch. There was no way I was ditching my Choos. My life as the daughter of a billionaire,yes-the shoes—not a chance in hell. I left my hair loose and tonged it into slight waves.

Grabbing a sky-blue colored purse—I wore no black outside of work—I opened my apartment door ready to catch a bus down to the strip. I'd get a cab home later.

Letting myself out of the apartment, I took a deep breath. *Come on Mila, it's one night. What's the worst that can happen? A sore head tomorrow?* I had the day off anyway.

If only I'd known...

CHAPTER
Four

Louis

Saturday 31 March 2018

We walked into my room at the MGM Grand. I'd booked each of us a King room, all paid for by one of my sponsors who thought the idea of us coming here was golden. The sheer size of the room was incredible with its bed, desk, couch, large TV, and huge bathroom.

"I can't believe we got one of these each." Max scrubbed a hand through his blonde curls.

"Yeah, well, if you get lucky with the ladies I don't wanna be hearing it." I laughed. "Plus, I need a place to bring my wife back to."

"You still on with that ridiculous idea?" Cam,

who I have to say was the most sensible of the bunch, though not *that* sensible, stared at me from under his floppy brown fringe.

"Duh? That's why we're here, Bro. To find me a wife. And on that note. What are we doing still in the rooms? Let's get our shit together and get out there." I walked over and high-fived each one. "Operation *Marrying Mrs Clayton* is on."

"Bloody hell. We don't even need to leave the hotel. This makes our hotels and shopping centres look like a model village." Cam gasped. He was right, there was a map in the lobby to show us where things were. The place was enormous.

"Well. I say we stay here tonight and look around the place." I switched my phone onto record.

"Hey there, everyone. We're here live from the MGM Grand. Earlier you saw our rooms, now we're going to show you some of the hotel. And what can I say? The place is vast. Absolutely enormous. Now as I've said to you before, this video is likely to end up 18+ and so for that reason I've put warnings all over the channel, so mum's you might want to watch this one yourself. Right, so on that note here we have the Lobby Bar so we're going to make our way inside and try it out."

And we did, and then we tried the bar called

Whiskey Down and then we hit the casino. I recorded us at various locations but the rest of the time we just let our hair down and enjoyed our hotel.

"Okay. Where next?" Jonno demanded, his red hair adding to his look of devilment.

"Let's go to the nightclub." I started to walk in the direction of it and the rest of them followed.

"This place is fucking huge. We could fit the population of Leeds in here." Max's mouth had fallen open.

"Let's get some drinks." I gestured to the bar.

We had a few beers and then it was time to hit the floor. "Come on, time for me to search for a wife." The place was loud and bustling and I wasn't sure I'd be able to hear what any potential wife said to me, but I'd give it a go.

Max immediately zeroed in on a hot blonde and that left me facing her friend who had her back turned to me. She was bound to be butt ugly. It's how it went.

Then she turned around.

Oh. My. Fucking. God.

Her long dark hair swished around her face as she danced, lost in the music. She was wearing a white dress which due to the heat clung to her body giving me a large hint of what lie beneath—an amazing pair of tits. As she looked up, I saw her eyes were green and her mouth looked like it needed to be fastened on mine, just as she launched in my direction.

"Why don't I do this more often?" She asked.

CHAPTER
Five

Mila

A few hours earlier...

"Oh my God, I cannot believe you brought me here." I shouted over the very loud noise huge groups of women were making. We were at the Excalibur waiting for *Thunder from Down Under* to come on stage.

"Hey, we needed to start the evening right, girl." Jenny laughed. She'd ordered herself a Black Russian while I'd gone for a glass of white wine, which had elicited an eye-roll.

"Can I just tell you that there's no playing it safe tonight. We're to be that slammed we don't know which way is up. I have an urge to party." Jenny said, and she whooped as the men walked on stage.

Loud catcalls came from the audience as the men danced to *Uptown Funk*. I was used to a noisy bar, but these women were wildcats.

The men performed stunts and gymnastics and changed outfits several times going from firemen to cowboys to a SWAT team. Any woman's fantasy, they performed it. I was pleased that we weren't too near the front as I watched one of the men spray champagne out of his mouth in a fountain all over the women, who screamed like he'd showered them in diamonds.

"That's just gross." I pulled a face.

Jenny called over a waitress. "Honey, could we have six tequila shots here please?" She turned to me and waved a hand over me like I was Cinderella pre-Prince and glamor. "This shit stops now. You will down the tequila and we will party."

I sighed and sat back, thinking about my situation. I was twenty-three, it was Saturday night in Vegas, and I was acting like I had a stick up my ass.

The tray of shots came, and I picked one straight up. "Come on then, let's get the party started." I yelled, and we drank the drinks in quick succession. I choked a little and my eyes watered but I just giggled. "If I get into any trouble this evening, you have to pay my bail money, okay? We've all watched *The Hangover*. We know how this can go wrong."

"Nothing will go wrong. We're gonna have a good time and maybe get laid."

It was at that point I realized a man from the troupe was making his way over to us. Tall with long dark hair he was wearing a tank and pants. He stood in front of me and gave a hip thrust in my direction. "Go for it, Mila." Jenny yelled.

The guy dragged me to my feet and danced with me, pulling me toward his groin. Then he sat me back down on my chair and ripped his tank in half in front of me revealing an oil-slicked chest. His pants were next, ripped off leaving him in just some tiny briefs. He continued to hip thrust at me and I smiled and yelled like I was supposed to. I could have a good time. The guy was hot, and the tequila was starting to melt my reserves. I almost lost my voice I screamed so loud for the rest of the show, but the tequila helped.

"Jenny, I want to dance."

"I know just the place." She said. "Come on."

We entered Hakkasan at the MGM Grand. I didn't

think I'd ever get used to the size of all these places. There were floor maps as you walked in because the hotels were that huge. The MGM had several bars, a shopping area, a theater... You name it, it was there. But best of all I decided when I walked inside the place, was the nightclub. A large screen faced us with smaller screens underneath, all showing patterns that matched the beat of the music the DJ was playing. He stood on his large podium in front of the screens.

"Let's dance." I mouthed at Jenny and we headed for the middle of the floor where we let the music take over.

The night went on.

Dance.

Drink.

Dance.

Drink.

You get the message.

My dress was almost stuck to my body, but I didn't care. I was having the time of my life.

"Why don't I do this more often?" I yelled at Jenny, then I realized, it wasn't Jenny.

I moved my head slowly. Where the fuck had my friend gone? Then I saw her at the side of me dancing with a guy with short blond curly hair. So who had I spoken to?

I let my head fall back a little so I could better focus on the guy in front of me. Dark hair, reeeeaallly dark eyes. His cheekbones, whoa! They were intense, like they'd been carved out of rock, and his lips, mmmm plump.

"You know you are feeling my face, right, love?" He said in a strange accent.

I pointed at him. "You're British?"

"Yep, sure am, and you're American."

"That's right. You're so clever." I giggled. "What's your name and do you know Prince Harry because there's time for him to call the wedding off you know?"

"Sorry, I spoke to Harry just last night, and he's definitely going ahead with it."

I sighed. "Pity. Are you single?" I grabbed hold of his hands. No rings. That was good.

"I am."

"No girlfriend? Boyfriend?"

"Totally available."

I touched his face again. "Are you real because I've had a lot to drink?"

He laughed and his face just got even better

looking. I couldn't stop staring and was amazed my body was still dancing.

"So are you on holiday?" He asked me. It was difficult to hear him and I kept having to get very close to him. I realized I kept scrunching up my eyes and wondered how that was helping me hear him better.

"No. I live here and work at *Little Black Dress*."

"What's that? A clothes shop?"

I clutched my stomach and laughed, then I mimicked his British accent but tried to do it like the Queen. "Ay-clothes-shoppe. Are you on vacation?" I asked him, "or did I make a wish and you went 'poof' from your house to my night out?"

"I'm Louis." He said still dancing. I watched his hips gyrate. Holy fuck!

"Mila." I shouted back. Then I danced with him, all sexy, up close and personal. My evening was sure going well. I glanced over to Jenny who gave me a thumbs up.

I loved Jenny, I decided. She was the most best friend forever-ever because this night was amazing.

The guy I was dancing with kept holding his cell up and filming us dancing and chatting but I didn't care. If he wanted something to remember me by, so be it. Anyway, he was gorgeous, and I was in love.

"What are you looking for?" He asked me, an amused smirk on his lips.

"Cupid."

"Cupid?"

"Yeah. He must be here somewhere."

Hot guy grabbed me and pulled me closer. "Yeah, I guess he must be."

We carried on dancing.

CHAPTER Six

Mila

April 1st, 2018 - Sunday

I woke up, my face smooshed into my pillow. My head pounded and my mouth was so dry. I slowly sat myself up and then screamed because I wasn't at home.

"Jeez, keep it down." A male voice came from my left-hand side. I slowly slid my eyes over to that side of the bed. Fuck! It was hot guy from last night, and he had no clothes on his top half. What about his bottom half?

I very, very slowly lifted the sheet up to look at my own body. Yup. Not a stitch of clothing, and then the memories from the night before started to hit, like someone throwing me a jigsaw to assemble but with pieces missing. But one thing I did remember.

His massive cock.

My pussy throbbed in recollection.

I brought my hand to my face and rubbed at my left eye where a pain throbbed behind it. Something hard hit me in the eye.

Fuck what was on my hand?

I held my left hand up in front of me, feeling all the blood drain from my face.

On my left hand, on my wedding finger... was a wedding ring.

Oh dear God, no!

I pushed at the body at the side of me.

"You. You there. I need to talk to you. Sit up, it's an emergency."

A sigh escaped the body and then he stretched out. Muscled arms stretched from the covers, a slight hint of the man chest. My core went slick.

Stop it. We need all body processes to the brain right now.

An eye opened and then another.

"Hey there, wifey."

Wifey?

I swallowed. "Could you please tell me what's

going on, because I'm only remembering parts of last night?"

He looked shocked. "Which parts?"

"Well I mainly remember one big one." I nodded my head toward where I imagined his crotch would be underneath the comforter.

He laughed and once again I was struck by how gorgeous he was. At least I'd drunk married a hottie.

"You don't remember proposing? Or the wedding?"

A flash of a retro jukebox came to mind followed by an image of Tyrion Lannister from Game of Thrones.

"No."

Those dark eyes bored into mine. "Oh. I feel a little offended that you don't remember our nuptials."

"I don't even remember your name, never mind marrying you." My voice was getting higher in pitch with every word I uttered.

"Louis. My name is Louis, Mrs. Clayton."

Him calling me Mrs. Clayton hit me like the implosion of the Riviera Hotel.

My eyes scanned the door. I wanted to run. I escaped from the bed having spotted my purse in the corner of the room. Where was my phone? Where was Jenny?

In my haste the whole fact I was entirely naked completely escaped me until the air conditioned air hit my flesh, making me shiver and my nipples pebble.

"Come back to bed, Mrs. Clayton." Oh my God even his voice was sexy.

"I need to phone my friend and see what happened to her. You know I'm not a good friend, right? Friends don't leave their friends and go get married. Nu-huh."

"Relax. She's in the room next door with my mate, Max."

My gaze lifted to his.

"No they didn't get hitched."

I stood in the middle of the room in my birthday suit. What did I do now? I needed all the details of what happened, and then I had to find out how to get an annulment. What had I gotten myself into?

"I love that tattoo by the way." He said, nodding in the direction of my ass. "Didn't taste of anything but body lotion though when I bit it."

Staring at my new husband lying there with his come-to-bed eyes I decided fuck it, both mentally and literally.

Might as well make the best of a situation, right?

"Okay, I'm coming back to bed. Maybe some more memories will come back if we do it again."

Louis pushed that gorgeous mouth out in a mock pout. "I'm hurt. I remember everything."

"You do?"

"Yeah, I was merry, but I wasn't wasted like you must have been. I mean, I knew you were pretty drunk, but you seemed to know what you were doing."

Moving back across the room, I climbed under the duvet. "I clearly had no idea what I was doing, and I've decided the time to be sensible about the situation is not right now." I snaked my hand across the bed trying to find his cock and see if it was definitely as large as I remembered.

Oh yeah!

"I thought you'd be out of the door seeking an immediate annulment." Louis raised an eyebrow.

"First fact of our married life. Your wife is unpredictable."

I could remember the beginning of the evening and dancing with Louis for ages. It was after that everything went vague.

I moved in closer.

"Second fact, Mrs. Clayton gives amazing head."

I threw the covers off us and took him in my mouth.

It wasn't easy. He was huge, but I was a pro at a blow.

Sitting astride him, I looked up from my position to the top of the bed. Louis' eyes were closed, small groans coming from his mouth. I sucked harder, taking him to the back of my throat.

"Oh fuck, yes."

Hollowing out my cheeks I bobbed my head back and forth, blowing him for all I was worth until he exploded into my mouth. I swallowed and moved back over to my side of the bed.

"Your turn." My new husband said, and he moved down the bed. He pushed my thighs apart and his warm breath ghosted over my core and then his tongue flicked up my seam and I almost came off the bed.

"So wet for me." He said, and that was the last of his words. Instead he used that tongue to flick across my nub rapidly, causing a bunch of sensations at my core. I pushed against him and his tongue moved to lick up my seam and dart inside me.

"Oh, oh, oh."

He returned to my clit and pushed fingers inside me, twisting them this way and that while his expert tongue worked me, until I felt the pressure build and I came against his face. To be honest, I was surprised he didn't need a lifeguard I was that wet.

As he moved up my body, I felt his cock against my thigh. It was hard—again.

He moved over me and pushed against my heat. I gasped as he filled me to the hilt.

"So fucking tight."

I doubted I was, this wasn't my first rodeo, but I guess I'd seem so with that beast pushing inside me. I felt strangely proud that my pussy seemed fit. Maybe the three Kegel exercises I'd performed in my life had done something after all?

Then all thoughts, rational or otherwise, were forgotten as he thrust inside me while he kissed and sucked at my neck.

"Oh yeah, oh yeah. Please. Now. Now."

He let out a huge groan as he came inside me and my pussy contracted around his cock. God, there were no words to how good it felt. An annulment could wait. I was going to shag my sexy new husband senseless.

I'd already lost mine.

Jenny had sent me a text saying she was going straight home from the hotel and would catch up with me later and was I regretting my actions yet?

I sent a quick text back saying I'd not yet had time to regret them with a wink emoticon followed by an aubergine emoticon.

After eating pizza in bed ordered via room service, I headed to the shower. Once dried and dressed, I looked over at Louis.

"So I'm gonna get going. Could you give me your details: cell number, home address, full name—anything else you think I might need?" I picked up a complimentary hotel pen and swiped a page off the matching note pad and scrawled on my info.

"This is me so you can get hold of me. It was nice being married to you for a day and if you want to hit me up for more honeymoon sex while you're here then my cell number is there, although after tonight I'll be working. In fact I'll put my shifts on here too."

Louis watched me with that amused smirk back atop his lips.

"What?" I pouted at him.

"Just wondering if getting married was the craziest thing I ever did or whether that would be getting the annulment?" He said.

"I wish I could remember the damn wedding." I

replied. "Trust me to forget the most important day of my life." I giggled. "I'll be seeing ya, Louis Clayton."

"You will." Louis winked.

I caught a cab back to my apartment and changed straight into some comfy pajamas. I curled up on the couch, pulling a blanket over me, my head on a couple of cushions and I tried to think about what I could remember from the evening before.

Thunder from Down Under. I could remember all of that.

The nightclub. I could remember parts of that, mainly dancing.

Then what did we do? I couldn't remember leaving but had a vague recollection of being hungry.

Yes! We grabbed a burger.

Then it was a blur apart from the jukebox playing Love me Tender, and this recollection of Tyrion Lannister. Only now I was remembering a very small Elvis too.

I leaned onto the floor where I'd put my purse and took my cell out of my bag, dialing Jenny's number.

"Well, finally the newlywed emerges."

"Jen. What the fuck happened?"

There was a pause. "What do you mean what happened? You don't remember?"

"I remember the naked men, and the dancing with a hot guy. Then I remember you dancing with a blond one. I'm guessing that's who you were with? Max, I think Louis said he was called."

"Yeah, we had fun. I'm not seeing him again though. I got fed up of the constant recording of everything. His phone was never out of his hand."

"Recording? What was he recording?"

"They were all recording various parts of the evening. Louis is a YouTuber. Did he not tell you? They're recording their trip as he's trying to hit a million subscribers. Apparently he's going to do something epic while he's here to try to break America and also to get the average age of his subscribers above fifteen. Well I guess they need to act older than three-year-old's then.

"So why did you go to the hotel with him if he was a chump?"

"I only shared his bed. I didn't do anything with him. Well, maybe we made out a little, but we were next door to you and I wanted to make sure you were okay before I left. To be honest, I expected you to have a meltdown, and that we'd leave together. I didn't think you'd actually stay with him all day."

"He had a massive cock, Jenny. Like an elephant trunk."

She laughed down the phone. "So you stayed for a repeat performance?"

"Absolutely. Several repeat performances."

It was then I remembered the date. "Fucking hell. Oh my God, you all really had me going there. It's April Fools' Day. You're supposed to have confessed by now. God, I'm suck an idiot. Totally fooled."

"Sorry, Mila. It would be easier to tell you it was an April Fool's but no, you really married him."

"I did? Oh crap." That was that sense of relief obliterated.

"So now what are you going to do?"

"Now I get an annulment and carry on with my life, although I'm hoping to see him again while he's still here. I just wish I could remember more of what happened."

"Oh, Mila. Didn't you get what I was saying? They were recording. Louis. Is. A. YouTuber. I'd expect a video upload in the next few hours about the whole thing."

There was a silence while I gathered my

thoughts. "Pardon? You mean to tell me my evening's exploits are going to be uploaded on YouTube?"

"I would have thought so. In the meantime, go catch up on who you just married. Louis Clayton. YouTube channel: Clayton's Classics."

Dread pooled in my stomach. "How bad is it on a scale of one to ten?"

"I'm saying nothing. Call me tomorrow. I'm here if you need me to help with any paperwork."

She ended the call. I swung my legs off the couch and went to grab my laptop. It was time to familiarize myself with my new husband's career and wait to see if the night became any clearer when I viewed it all on my screen.

What had I done?

CHAPTER
Seven

Mila

My new husband does not only have a giant cock, he IS a giant cock.

A week ago he spent a stupid amount of money buying fries to see if he could win a great prize in a competition. He won more fries.

He has ridden a skateboard in a supermarket. Also, a scooter.

He has sat in a bath of cold beans.

He has eaten extremely hot chillies.

All for the sake of having some kind of 'fame' and it would appear to be working because he had plenty of sponsorship and subscribers. But his latest vlog is where things got really 'rip my own hair out'. I pressed play to watch his latest video again.

"Well, hello there, everyone. We're here live from

the MGM Grand. Earlier you saw our rooms, now we're going to show you some of the hotel. And what can I say? The place is vast. Absolutely enormous. Now as I've said to you before, this video is likely to end up 18+ and so for that reason I've put warnings all over the channel, so mum's you might want to watch this one yourself. Right, so on that note here we have the Lobby Bar so we will make our way inside and try it out."

It then cut to them drinking in another bar and then them going into a casino. The camera was fixed on Louis' face as he chatted away. *"Well, I can certainly see that my luck isn't in tonight in terms of gambling, but that's not why we're here anyway guys is it? We can't tell you our big secret yet, but we are here for a reason, and all shall become clear if I manage to pull it off and no, that's not a euphemism."*

A big secret? Some other childish prank no doubt. His mother must be so proud.

While I watched, a new video came up on the sidebar. My eyes went out on stalks at the headline.

I GOT MARRIED IN VEGAS! MEET MRS. CLAYTON!

My breath came in short pants and I thought I would pass out. *Please tell me I'm not going to find myself the main subject of a YouTube video watched by almost a million subscribers?* Not when I was drunk out of my mind. And how much of my wedding is on there, given I can barely remember the evening at all?

I felt sure I would be sick.

My cell phone rang and I answered Jenny's call.

"There's a new video. Do you want me to come round? We can watch it together? Only it's quite long and we may need to pause and chat."

"Why would we need to pause and chat?"

"Max called me. It was Louis' plan. To get married in Vegas for his channel. You're likely to go viral, babes."

I closed my eyes and sucked on my top lip.

"Get a cab straight over and bring lots of alcohol."

Y

Forty minutes later, Jenny walked in and shrugged off her jacket, leaving it on the back of a dining room chair. "I have wine. Oh you have glasses ready. Good girl." She opened the bottle and began to pour.

"Fill that baby right up. The video already has 543,000 views, Jenny. Over half a million people have seen my wedding who are not me. I need to get this watched so we can decide on my next course of action."

I pressed play and there he was heading into the nightclub.

"This place is epic."

"Look how many people are here, bro." One of his friends said. *"There's bound to be someone here."*

Footage followed of them getting drinks and dancing and then all of a sudden there me and Jenny were on screen.

"Oooh, I'm on YouTube." Jenny squealed with excitement.

"Really?" I shot her a side-eye, and she shrugged and mumbled 'sorry' at me.

The camera panned in on me and Louis. You couldn't hear what we were saying because it was one of the others filming at this point but what you could see was the mutual attraction between us. It was off the charts and on the screen.

"Whoa. You are undressing him with your eyes there, babes."

"He is HOT." I said. "Just a shame he's a jerk."

Then it's Louis holding the camera, and he's talking to me while we're on screen. *"So this is Mila. I think you're going to agree with me that she's absolutely gorgeous."*

"Awww thank you." I say as I push him, so he staggers slightly.

Jeez, I was wasted.

"So we've spent," he looks at his watch, *"the last hour together and well, folks, I'm in love. My mother was always going on about this instalove she reads about in books and I'd laugh at her. Well, Mum, I think you were right after all. I know I'm going to marry this girl."*

"You're going to marry me?" I say. *"When?"*

"I don't know. When shall we get married?"

"How about tonight? How about we get married right now?" My face breaks out into a huge beaming smile. I look down at my dress. *"Look, I already have the dress on. It's white and has lace."*

"Perfect." He shouts.

"Oh my fucking God, that dress is stuck to my body with sweat. You can totally see my rack." I turned to Jenny.

"Stop talking. I don't want to miss a second of this."

I pressed pause.

"Do you not remember this either? You were there?"

"No, I wasn't." She pointed to the screen and sure enough she's not in shot. "I was at the bar with Max. When we got back you were gone. When we finally found out what had happened, you were back at the hotel with your new husband, so I stayed there."

I pressed play.

"We need a ring." My husband-to-be announces and two other guys follow us out of the club. In the next scene we are choosing a ring in the MGM Grand's jewelry store.

"Hey, that ring of yours is worth a bit."

I stared at the diamond and gold band on my hand. "I thought it was fake. Thank God I didn't throw it in the trash can."

From there we're filmed in a cab riding to the Clark County Marriage Bureau and emerging with papers looking ecstatic. We can't stop kissing each other by this stage. It's mortifying to watch.

But not as mortifying as my wedding.

Louis has called several chapels and has found

one with a vacancy. The wedding was already booked, but the couple were a no-show so for a reduced fee we take the slot agreeing to use everything they already had prepared. So as we walk in to the chapel, we are greeted by a dwarf dressed as Tyrion Lannister, who stands behind a fridge containing alcohol.

"Your champagne is already paid for, let me get you all a drink while you wait for the ceremony." He said.

"It's not actually him off Game of Thrones is it?" I crinkled my eyes up trying to stare at the dwarf. I even bent down to his height. Lord have mercy.

After drinks we are taken through to the room where we are to be married. Is it a beautiful chapel bedecked with flowers? No, it's decorated like the inside of a spaceship. At one side is a table with some eclairs and donuts on it, and a jukebox (at which point all my remembered flashbacks have appeared).

And then 'Tyrion' came back in dressed as Elvis, but Elvis in a Star Trek costume. I watched in horror as me and Louis were married by mini-Elvis who then sang *Love me Tender* to us live. But it wasn't his singing making me cringe—it was me and Louis.

We were singing to each other. I didn't know all the words so then I made my own up.

"Love me tender, love me back in your rooooom." We kissed for about three minutes before we were informed it was all over and we had five minutes to eat a donut if we wanted one.

"So I'd like to present Mrs. Clayton to you." Louis stroked the side of my face. *"My lovely wife."*

"Your mum is gonna shit a brick." A male voice yelled in the background.

"You're gonna love her, Mum, she's soooo pretty."

"I have a new mom." I gasped. *"Got to be better than my old one."* I waved at the screen. *"Hey, new mom."*

"It's so funny how I say mum and you say mom." Louis said, then he kissed me again, the phone wobbling and us going out of view. You could just hear small groans and slurping noises.

At this point I am watching the screen from behind my hand, my fingers outstretched.

Limos were provided as part of the wedding package and we all climbed inside.

"Well you did it." A guy with red-hair said. *"Aim achieved. You married a stranger in Vegas."*

"Ssshh." The other guy said, to an eye-roll from the redhead.

"I am a very happily married man." Louis announced. *"Very happy indeed."*

"I am a very happily married woman." I replied.

The video closed on us going into Louis' room. Thank. Actual. God.

He closed the door with a wink on his face.

Then the screen faded to black.

Just as I thought it was finished his face returned to the screen.

"So," Louis said looking at the screen. *"Well, as you may have worked out. I came to Vegas to do the ultimate prank—marry a stranger—and as you can see, I did."* He looked off screen and smiled. *"So what do you think? She's lovely isn't she?"* He laughed a great hearty laugh, and the video ended.

I threw myself on the floor dramatically, face down.

"My life is over." I mumbled into the carpet.

My cell beeped with an incoming text signal. I ignored it, then Jenny spoke.

"It's your husband. He wants to meet you to discuss what you do next."

"Next, I kill him for making me look an idiot in front of thousands of people."

"Millions." She says. "One-point-five-million views so far and he just hit a million subscribers."

I rolled over and stared at the ceiling.

"I thought I might really like him, Jenny. Like

reaaaalllly. But he's an idiot. An idiot who married me for a joke. And so now I'm the joke. I'm not happy."

Jenny leaned over and refilled my wine glass. "I wonder how famous he is? Whether or not the press will get hold of the story. You could end up famous."

"I don't want attention. I hate attention. Been there, done that." I thought about all the photographers who had wanted to capture photos of Walt Williams, one of the richest men in New York, and the times I was told to look pretty and smile for the camera. If it got out who I'd just married, it would make my father a laughing stock.

"How do I get hold of the UK press?" I asked Jenny.

CHAPTER
Eight

PULSE ONLINE

Your one stop shop for celebrity gossip

MONDAY 2 APRIL 2018

BREAKING NEWS

Walt Williams' errant daughter and heir, Mila, marries UK YouTube Sensation Louis Clayton in Vegas.

It's presently unclear whether a genuine spontaneous wedding, or a prank for his channel.

UPDATES TO FOLLOW.

CHAPTER Nine

Louis

<u>Sunday 1 April 2018</u>

When my new wife woke up a few hours after our impromptu wedding, I don't know what I expected but it certainly wasn't a blow job. And boy was it a good one. Mila had mad skills.

So of course it would have been shady of me not to return the oral favour.

I sighed when I thought of all the hot sex we'd enjoyed, followed by pizza, and easy conversation.

I don't think I could have found a better wife if I'd been dating someone for two years as who I'd found in two hours. This was ridiculous. I began berating myself. It was lust, pure and simple. Not love. Just luck that I'd found a hot babe who gave great head.

I stared at my wedding ring. I'd never had any jewellery before, now I had an eighteen-carat gold ring around my wedding finger. But although I kept playing with it as it felt unusual on my hand, I kind of liked it.

Last night I had drunk plenty, but I'd obviously not been as pissed up as my wife as at least I remembered getting married—and consummating the wedding. I mean did she not remember that too? It had been a bit of a quickie because by that point we'd almost dry humped each other to death, but still —bit of a knock to the system if she couldn't remember it. I'd have to ask her, maybe. Perhaps it was better not to know?

The guys had been around my room now for a couple of hours and we were getting the video ready to upload, having had to edit it from different phones and what the chapel had given us. It had been surreal to watch the wedding sober. I couldn't believe I'd actually done it.

"Well, your ratings are about to go through the roof. I'm sure." Max said. "Are we gonna get room service and lots of booze and sit and watch what happens?"

"Of course!" I stretched out on the mattress, my head on the pillow. "It's uploading. Pass the room service menu, Cam. All that sex today has made me ravenous."

Three sets of eyes looked at me with envy.

"So what's next then? Just get an annulment?" Jonno asked.

"I would imagine so. I need to arrange to meet her to sort it all out. She's given me her phone number. But tonight lets just see what happens once the vlog hits and not worry about silly little things like me being legally wed to a fit bird."

"Yeah my heart bleeds." Jonno said. "Oh by the way," he added. "You got your mobile phone nearby?"

"Yeah, why?"

It began ringing. "That's why."

I looked at the caller ID - my mother.

Shit.

"Hey, Ma."

"Don't you 'hey ma' me, you stupid child. Did I not bring you up with a brain in your head? I blame that bloody father of yours. Always making me the bad parent and letting you get away with murder. 'Leave him be, Janet. The boy's got to learn.' What have you just learned now then? I'll tell you. Number one: only complete tools would marry someone they only just met, and number two: only a complete dickhead—and yes you're making your own mother be very rude—would get married WITHOUT THEIR MOTHER PRESENT."

I held the phone out away from my ear because she'd just fried it with her ranting. She was so loud the guys could hear every word and were rolling around laughing. Yeah, thanks for the support there.

"Mum, it's not a proper wedding. It's just for the channel."

"Oh." She quietened down. "So it's fake then? Bloody hell, it looked real. Did you have to pay the actress? She was very good at acting drunk I have to say."

"Erm, no. The ceremony was legit and legal, but I'd only just met Mila earlier that night. I'm going to see her about getting an annulment."

"Did you consummate the wedding, son?"

"Mother!"

"That's a yes. I go back to my original statement. YOU'RE A COMPLETE DICKHEAD. Now I love you, but sort this out ASAP."

With that she hung up on me.

"How long before those beers get here?"

We watched as the views kept climbing higher, and higher, and then it happened.

ONE MILLION SUBSCRIBERS.

I immediately did another video.

"Oh my God. Thank you so much guys. We just hit one million subscribers. That is amazing. Beyond my wildest dreams. We're here now, the four of us, just chilling in my room. We have room service ordered, the beers will be here soon so we can celebrate more. But it's over to you. How do you want us to celebrate this milestone? Giveaways? You tell us. Please if you've liked the videos hit like. Don't forget if you haven't already to subscribe, and comment below with what we should do to celebrate."

I logged off and then we watched as the comments came in.

There was the usual. Win a meet with us. Give away an Xbox. But one thing came up ten times more than any other suggestion.

We want to see more of Mila.

"Holy shit. They want to see the missus. How are you going to deliver on that one seeing as you're getting an annulment?"

I chewed the side of my lip. The fact remained

57

that we were here another five days yet, and I had an opportunity to spend a lot of that time having wildly hot sex if Mila was game. I was going to have to meet her, confess all and then see if I could get her on board with extending her time as Mrs Clayton. Just until the end of my trip.

Because my fans wanted it...

And I'd have been lying if I hadn't have admitted that I wanted it too.

So I picked up my phone and sent her a text. We needed to meet.

Monday 2 April 2018

The next morning I woke to loud banging on my door. Fuck, what was on fire?

I staggered over to the interconnecting door, opened it, and watched as Jonno almost fell through it.

"You fucking top lad. Do you know who you married?"

He flung his phone in my face.

And there she was, in a family photo.

I shook my head. "I don't understand."

"Read the article, you dipshit. I didn't give it you so you could get a stiffy over the photo."

I read on and discovered my new wife was heiress to billions of pounds… but estranged from her parents.

"Yeah. I don't give a shit about any of that." I told him.

"Are you for real? She makes friends with daddy and you stay with her and you're set for life, man. Set. For. Life. And of course you wouldn't forget your friends would you, so we'd all be quids in?"

"Like you need any more money. You're bloody loaded." Jonno was a property developer.

"Never say no to more."

"I wonder why she's estranged from them?" I scratched my chin.

"Well, they're saying she came to Vegas with another bloke who ripped her off. Only wanted her for her money. They disowned her, so she stayed."

I find my shoulders and jaw setting tight at the thought of a previous boyfriend.

"They sound like jerks. She's better off without them. So, anyway." I said. "I'm meeting her today at the bar. What are you three going to get up to?"

"We're doing the helicopter ride over the Grand Canyon."

"Seriously?" My jaw dropped.

"Are we fuck? We're getting wasted and hitting more casinos. Do you know us at all?" He slapped my back. "Good luck with the missus and remember billions. Not millions. Billions." He mimed sharing out money from his hand.

I rolled my eyes. "Get out of here and try not to go bankrupt while I'm gone."

"Try not to break your dick off with all the shagging."

"We're going to talk."

This time it was Jonno's turn to eye-roll.

I walked in to the Millennium hotel and caught the lift up to the first floor where the *Little Black Dress* bar was situated. The place was classy, and I felt seriously under-dressed in my jeans and tee but as I looked around, I saw other customers dressed the same, though most seemed to be men in business suits and women in party dresses. The walls were a rich, dark wood colour; the carpets red, and all the door furniture was gold. That gold extended out into the rest of the decor. The name of the bar became clear when I approached the counter and every waitress who stood behind was wearing exactly that. Short little black dresses. Some were daring, some were lacy, all were sexy.

A throat cleared behind me and I spun around.

Mila.

The other wait staff faded from my mind like I had instant and severe memory loss.

She stood there in her little black dress. It was like a second skin on her body, and there were cutouts at each side of her waist. The neckline dipped into a V, just showing the top of those fantastic tits of hers, but oh so very sexy for the fact they didn't show any more than that hint.

My cock strained against my jeans at the sight of her. Her long dark hair was tied up in a ponytail, her green eyes fixed on mine.

"Hey, hubby." She said, and she grinned.

"Wife."

"So where shall we go? We need somewhere quiet right to talk? So we certainly need to be away from the *LBD*."

"I think we should see if this hotel has any rooms free." I ran my gaze up from her feet to her head, lingering over those perky breasts.

She repeated my exact eye movements, but her eyes lingered on my cock.

"Sounds like a plan." She replied, turning on her heel.

I had to watch her walk out into the lobby, following as that amazing ass sashayed from side to side. How I managed to not come in my pants I do not know.

I do know that we weren't a second through that hotel room door before I was buried inside her as she rode my cock like she was winning at the rodeo. It looked like conversation was going to have to wait.

CHAPTER
Ten

Mila

April 2nd, 2018 - Monday

Oops. We were in bed again. Oh, who was I kidding? I didn't care. A hot man who knew how to give a good time was in my bed. Excuse me if I didn't run off down to the courthouse to get rid of him.

Louis was lying on the left side of the bed facing me. I moved, so I was facing him. We both had the duvet tucked under our chins.

"You need to let me pay for my half of this room."

He shook his head. "No need. My sponsors are covering my expenses."

"Yeah, you need to tell me all about this

YouTube thing. So I married you because I was drunk and you married me for a stunt?"

He shuffled up the bed and placed his head back against the headboard.

I lifted myself up and stretched, making sure I was still under the covers.

"Do you fancy a coffee? Then we can talk."

"Sure." I watched as Louis got out of bed and took in the view of his fine peachy ass as he headed for the bathroom. He came back out after a few minutes wearing a robe and passed one to me. I slipped it on as he made us both a drink.

"I really should know how my wife takes her coffee."

"Strong. Plenty of milk, no sugar. How about you?"

"Rarely drink it, but medium strength, medium milk, no sugar."

"See, now we know."

He passed me my drink and crawled back into bed.

"So, how much do you know? Did you Google me? Watch the channel?"

"I watched some of the channel." I bit my lip and looked down at the duvet, finding a pulled thread fascinating.

"It's okay. It doesn't show my best side does it?"

I caught his gaze. "Well, I was kind of surprised. I mean, I know I don't remember a lot of the evening, but you weren't acting stupid or doing dumb tricks. Well, not until our wedding ceremony anyway."

"Yeah, well, about that." He scratched at his chin. "I'm trying to move away from the pranks; thing is the sponsors love them. They make money and I make money. I want to keep my channel because I have a huge amount of views."

"And your million subscribers. Congratulations by the way."

He beamed. "Thanks. I can't believe over a million people are interested in what I do. But I'm twenty-five now and something's got to change."

My brow creased. "So, what did you think? I need to grow up so I'll get married?"

He sighed. "I thought I needed a more grown up prank, but really… I don't know. I think I had an idea and all of us guys got carried away with the thought of a paid holiday to Vegas. Then alcohol got involved and here we are."

"Yeah, here we are. So, how do we get an annulment?"

"Well." I watched as he visibly swallowed. "I

wondered if you'd stay married to me... for another five days."

I spilled a bit of my coffee on the comforter.

"Stay married?"

"Yeah, only you were a complete hit on the channel. I don't know if you saw my vlog asking for what people wanted?"

"Yeah."

"Well, they said they wanted to see more of you."

I scoffed. "Me? Why would they want to see more of me? I'm no one special."

"Well, I'd have to disagree with that because I came to Vegas to look for a wife and chose you."

"Lucky me."

"Sorry that came out wrong. I meant above everyone else, you were the woman who caught my eye. The people on my channel must think the same thing."

"So what would I have to do?"

"Just hang with me. Show me some of Vegas maybe? I'm sorry the guys might be part of the package at times."

"Is the other package included?" I nodded in the area of his impressive dick.

"Of course. You can have that anytime. Married to me or not. Just call me." He burst into laughter.

"And so what's in this for me?"

"Apart from my company and my cock? You'll get sponsorship. There are already girls asking where your dress is from. It's five days. Why don't we just see what happens? Then at the end of the week, I'll go back to the UK and I'll sort the annulment."

I placed my coffee down, wriggled under the covers and stared at the ceiling.

He leaned over me.

"What are you thinking?"

"Advantages and disadvantages. So for example advantages are maybe new clothes. Disadvantage, having to hang around with four smelly boys for the rest of the week.

"Also there's the potential press interest. My Vegas exploits have hit the news. Which surprises me. Not in the UK because there's a journo there who is always ripping the shit out of me for my pranks and apparent bad influence on teenagers. But here in the US I didn't really expect to be on any news channels."

"I may have randomly called one with some hot gossip." I admitted.

"You did? Why?"

"I hate my family. It's the perfect opportunity to

wind them up. Sorry. So you see I'm getting as much out of this union as you are."

"Ah yeah, Jonno told me about you being some heiress who ran to Vegas with a boyfriend."

"I thought he was a boyfriend. He was actually a leech."

"Well I can assure you, I'm not a leech."

I shrugged. "It wouldn't matter anyway. I'm disowned."

"Surely your parents would welcome you back with open arms if you approached them?"

I glared at him. "Showing that you've obviously not met them and know nothing about the situation."

"Hey, hey, hey." He stroked a hand down my cheek. "Is this our first fight?"

I snickered. "If you think this is me fighting you really don't know me at all."

He moved over me pulling my robe apart. "So let's spend five more days with me getting to know you then? I'm going to start by finding out all your likes and dislikes." He threw his robe on the floor.

How was I supposed to say no to that?

He turned me over so my face was in my pillow, my butt facing him and he slapped my butt cheek.

"Ow, what's that for?" I asked, wriggling my butt up at him.

He spanked it again. "Hmm, I'm putting that in my brain as a like. You clenched your thighs together."

Bringing his hand around under me he moved beside me and pulled me into his side. His hand dipped down between my thighs. "So wet. Do you like this?" He said and his finger very slowly tickled at my nub. My breath hitched. He dipped in and out of my wetness, bringing his finger back to my clit. I thrust my pelvis up as his fingers dipped inside me. "Yes. This is definitely another like."

Louis moved his finger further back. I knew where he was headed, and I tensed. "Hmmm, I'm guessing this is unchartered territory. We'll leave this one for now." I relaxed again. He was right. I'd never done that and the thought made me nervous.

Pushing me onto my back his head lowered between my thighs and once more he feasted on my pussy. God, I needed to come so bad.

He broke off lifting his head up and as my lusty gaze met his and saw his mouth dripping with my juices, he said. "This is a definite yes," before he returned to my core.

My pussy gave him his answer as I came hard all over his mouth. "Oh my God. Fuck, Louis."

"Oh, okay then. Seeing as you asked." He

replied, coming back and flipping me over, pulling me up onto my knees. He pushed in behind me, reaching out to grab one of my breasts. The other jiggled as he pushed in and out of my core. The only sound in the room was our lustful moans and rapid breathing.

"Fuck, I could do this all day and all night." Louis groaned out as he continued to thrust. I could feel my center tightening, ready to release again. Then Louis' pace quickened, and he thrust into me faster, harder. I pushed back against him with all the energy I had.

"Dirty girl." He whispered near me and that did it. I exploded, feeling Louis tighten and then join me. Our sweaty bodies collapsed on the bed, Louis rolling off me, to the side and then pulling me next to him once more.

"That's a yes for it hard and fast." He said.

"It's a yes to everything, Louis, with you. I can't get enough." I said.

His fingers trailed down the side of my cheek and brushed over my lips. "Yeah, I feel the same."

He moved away from me slightly, pushing up against the headboard once more. "This is just cos it's new, right, and we're attracted to each other?

That's why we're so damn horny and can't get out of bed."

"Yeah." I said agreeing. "What else would it be?"

He shuffled off the bed. "Just going to the bathroom."

He moved away, and I laid back thinking about my previous boyfriends. It had never been like this before. Ever. This connection was different. In fact that word summed it up. A connection. It was like we were meant to be. We just fit together. I couldn't tell him that though. We'd not known each other forty-eight hours yet.

This was crazy, and yet I couldn't stop it.

CHAPTER Eleven

Louis

It had never been like this before. Ever. I'd had many girlfriends, but it hadn't been like this. We'd not known each other forty-eight hours yet.

This was crazy, and yet I couldn't stop it.

I stood in the bathroom splashing my face with cold water, trying to get myself out of this. Out of what I was feeling. All I wanted to do was stay in this hotel room with this woman and lock the world out.

But I couldn't.

I'd come here with friends, via sponsors, for the channel.

I had to work, and I had to keep more of a distance from Mila. Remind myself that she was only with me because she got drunk and then saw me as an opportunity to get revenge on her parents.

I needed to remember that.

So, if she was willing, I would let her show us Vegas. I would record vlogs for the channel and then next Saturday morning, I would be gone. Back to my life in Leeds.

I rubbed at my stomach. It felt funny.

It felt like... disappointment.

Jesus, what the fuck was happening to me? I re-splashed my face with more water.

Come on, Louis. Get a grip, and not on her hips as you fuck her again.

My dick hardened with that thought.

My resolve dissolved.

I was leaving this bathroom to screw her again and then... then... I really needed to leave. Though the hotel was paid up until tomorrow lunchtime...

Tuesday 3 April 2018

I finally returned to my own hotel room in the early hours of Tuesday morning where I hit my bed and slept for hours. I'd turned my phone off so that the guys didn't disturb me. So when I woke at 10am and turned it back on, I wasn't surprised to see angry messages in our group chat. I sent a message that I was up and did everyone want to meet in my room. An hour later three pissed off faces joined me.

"You bring us to Vegas and then go off grid. Fuck us over for some pussy. What's going on, bro? This isn't on." Cam was livid. His cheeks red as he vented.

My jaw set. "Please don't call Mila 'pussy'. But you're right and I'm sorry. Let's go hang today and have some fun."

"So you sorted the annulment, or is she on board to stay married to you until the end of the week?" Jonno asked.

"We're staying hitched for now."

"Does that mean you're gonna be ditching us again?" Cam was still annoyed.

"I'm sure we can have the best of both worlds, but the subscribers and sponsors want more Mila. She's up for it, so that's what she gets. Let's not forget it's those subscribers and sponsors that are basically the reason we are here for free." I leveled Cam with a look and saw him nod.

"Yeah, I know. I was just looking forward to tearing it up in the city of sin."

"So what did you do last night?" I asked.

"You won't believe us." Max said. "We left the

evening's entertainment to Jonno to arrange..." He shook his head at him.

"It was on my bucket list." Jonno protested.

"What did you do?" I asked him.

"Erm, I made them come with me to watch Jennifer Lopez."

I collapsed back on the bed with laughter. "You gotta be shitting me?"

"Man, when she came onto that stage and stripped off to that little silver number with all the flesh showing underneath... blue balls. I got blue balls."

"The show started with her talking about giving the people all that she is and how she took the stairs not the elevator in life. There's two piles of puke from where me and Cam were sitting." Max added.

"No appreciation." Jonno pouted.

"We appreciated all the female supporting dancers didn't we, Cam?"

"Well I know what we're doing today guys." I'd been looking through my phone while they were chatting. "There's a beer festival."

The three annoyed faces I'd encountered cheered right up.

"Starts at 2pm, finishes at 7pm. So shall we go get a hearty breakfast ready to soak it all up?"

Mila had told me she was working from 2pm until 10pm at LBD. I'd not actually made any plans with her other than to say I'd message her, but after hours of drinking, me and the guys decided we'd go there. The guys were looking forward to seeing all the little black dresses.

"Whoa. This place is a bit posh isn't it?" Jonno said while his head swiveled around taking it all in.

"Sophisticated, yeah, so they might throw you out." I laughed. "Come on. Let's get a drink."

Max groaned. "Get me a scotch. Seriously no more beer. I'll burst."

We'd tried so many, and to be honest we were all a little bit wasted, but I wanted to see Mila. I put my phone on and started recording.

"Here we are in the Little Black Dress Bar at The Millennium Hotel. As you can see all the cocktail waitresses are in their little black dresses." I span the camera around to catch a few of them at work. *"And this one here, who in my opinion looks the best of all is Mila. Say hello, Mila."*

Mila spotted me and her eyes narrowed. "I'm guessing whatever you got up to today, alcohol was involved?"

"Could be. So Mila, could I have a slow, comfortable screw?"

Mila did an over-exaggerated sarcastic mock laugh. "Oh good one, I never heard that before. Actually why don't you try a Corpse Reviver? I think you need that more."

I picked up the cocktail menu off the bar with my other hand. *"Hmmmm, nope I think I'll have a hanky panky, or a bushwacker as I'd like to whack your bush."* I winked suggestively.

"The bathrooms are that way." Mila pointed.

I looked at her in confusion.

"Sorry, you pulled a face. I thought you were going to be sick."

"That was my come to bed face."

She scrunched up her nose. "I don't think it was."

"I'll have any of these: an orgasm, a slippery nipple or a quick fuck."

She sighed. "I think you need a coffee, Louis, and to grow up."

"You got a problem here, Mila? Only we're busy so if this jerk's annoying you I'll have him thrown out." A fat, balding bloke had walked up to Mila and put an arm around her while he stared at me menacingly. "And turn that fucking phone off."

Mila reached over, grabbed my phone and was

switching it off as I shouted, "I'm not a jerk. I'm her husband, so go fuck yourself."

The guy turned to Mila, who was rubbing at her forehead.

"Is this true? I didn't know you were married."

"We got married on Saturday." I shot back.

"It's complicated, Maximo." She told him. "But yeah if you can have security move him right now so that I can get on with my work, that would be appreciated."

"What? Mila. No."

"We'll take him with us. No need for security. Sorry, Mila." Jonno said. "We've been at a beer festival. We're all a bit merry. Some of us more than the others." He stared at me pointedly and then took my phone out of Mila's hand.

"Appreciated." Mila said and then she turned away from me.

"Don't you turn away from me, Mila Clayton. Mrs Mila Clayton." I shouted. "Do you hear me wife? Wife?"

A waitress with silver-blonde hair and freckles whipped around to look at Mila. "Did he just say you were his wife?"

"Not for much longer." Mila shouted, and then

security came over so I quit being a punk and followed Jonno out of the bar and back to the hotel.

I turned into a miserable drunk. Only Jonno stayed with me. The other two ditched me and went to gamble, saying that what with Jennifer Lopez and my pussy-whipped state, they were off out to properly enjoy a night in Vegas before it was too late.

Jonno made me coffee and left me to sleep.

Wednesday 4 April 2018

When I woke up I groaned as I remembered what I'd done, and fuck, I'd live-streamed half of it.

I picked up my phone to watch the playback and saw I had a text.

Mum: You are in so much trouble when you get home. That is NO WAY to treat a lady. I brought you up better than this! Apologise ASAP to that poor woman. You made a right show of her and a tit of yourself.

I flung my head back against the pillow. Then I found the stream and pressed play.

Oh my God. I had seriously fucked up. She was right. I really did need to grow up, and the first thing I needed to do was apologise.

I scrolled down to Mila's number and shot off a text.

Louis: Mila. I am so sorry. Are you at home? I'm coming to see you.

The reply came shortly after.

Mila: I think the only thing I need to see is papers for an annulment.
Louis: Please let me come and apologise.
Mila: I don't know.
Louis: I'd be bringing my penis with me...
There was a few minutes pause.
Mila: Okay. Give me an hour.

I drew up in the cab outside of the apartment block Mila lived in. There was a sign saying Springway over the entrance and I saw the pool straightaway. The place looked like somewhere you'd stay on your holidays, not somewhere to live.

I found the number of Mila's place and knocked. I heard footsteps approach and then the door opened. Mila stood there in white shorts and a baggy orange t-shirt, her hair tied up in a messy bun on the top of her head. She didn't have a scrap of make-up on and to me she looked more gorgeous than she did in her little black dress, or her white dress from our wedding for that matter.

I leaned in to kiss her, but she pulled away.

"I don't think so, Louis. We need to talk. Really talk."

Shit.

Following her inside I was directed to the small living room, and I took a seat on her couch.

"I'm just making coffee. You want one?" She hollered from the hallway.

"Yeah, please."

She brought them in a few minutes later and I felt strangely pleased that she'd remembered how I took it as I took a sip and tasted perfection.

She exhaled deeply. "Louis. I know your whole persona is based around being a jerk, but you brought that to my work place last night. That job is how I get to stay here, in this apartment. How I get to stay away from my parents. I can't have you coming in causing shit like that. Do you know how embarrassing it was having to tell my boss I got drunk married?"

My face scrunched up. "Well, why did you tell him that? Why not just say you got married, end of story? What business of his is it?"

"It's his business when I can't do my job properly and I wasn't telling him I got married like it was serious because it wasn't. It was a joke. I was drunk."

"But we got on? We had great sex."

She laughed. "You're being ridiculous now. You know this marriage is a sham and we need to end this now. Even though you have the most magnificent cock, I'm facing facts, and that is that in a couple of days you're going back to the UK and I will be here. Trying to save face over my drunken marriage. Summer heard. It went around the staff. Now they all know what I did Saturday night. I would have liked to have kept it quiet. No one there knew I was Mila Williams, heiress. They don't read the gossip because Vegas has enough of its own drama. You made me the drama. I'm pissed, Louis, and not in the way you Brits say it—like you were last night. What is it you say? Pissed up? You were out of control and it could have cost me everything."

I looked at the floor and then back up. "I'm so sorry, Mila. You are so right with everything. I do need to grow up. It's what I'm supposed to be doing with my channel. Last night I did loads of damage. Not just to you. I hurt my mum—again. And there's some serious abuse on the comments section on the channel."

"I don't give a crap about your channel, Louis. Who are all these people whose opinions you value so much? You don't know them. They don't know you. Is your self-worth so low its based around their opinions, or is your ego so huge you get off on the fact they are following your every move?"

I flinched at that comment.

"Yeah, thought so. It's your ego. Well I'm not impressed with the size of that."

"You like the size of something else."

"More jokes? Really? Did you look up the annulment?" Mila's jaw was set, she was steaming angry right now. Even offering my dick to her hadn't helped. I was in serious trouble.

I sighed. "Yes. We can fill a form in online for the County Clark family court. It takes about 20 days. Either of us can do it."

"Great. Let me get my laptop." She walked over

to the other side of the room and brought a laptop from her dining table.

This was sad. I knew our marriage was going to end, but I had hoped we'd make it to the end of the week. After this did it mean no more Mila in my life? I wanted to get to know her. Hell, I realised. I wanted to DATE her. In real life. Even though she lived in a different country.

Shit. I did not want this to end. I started to feel a bit nauseous and my heart started hammering in my chest.

She powered up the laptop and found the forms we needed and began to fill them in.

Now I felt like I had a stone lodged in my gut.

"Right. So the grounds for our annulment are that at the time of the ceremony you were mentally incompetent to make the decision." She told me.

I shook my head at her. "That's not true and it's on my channel as proof. I knew exactly what I was doing, so you'll have to be the mad one."

She glared at me, hands on her hips. "I am not declaring I was mentally incompetent."

"Well, we can't have an annulment then." I declared.

"Fine." She said. "I'll just have to look into getting

a divorce instead, due to irreconcilable differences or my husband being an A-hole who videos everything. I'm surprised you're not recording this." She flicked her hair. She looked adorable. I tried not to smile about the fact she couldn't get an annulment.

"So what do we do now then?" I asked.

"Well, we might as well go to bed." Mila declared. "But I've still not forgiven you, so it's going to be angry sex. I might even bite you or something."

She flounced off in the direction of the bedroom.

I hoped make-up sex followed the angry sex, but to be honest either was good with me right now. This woman was something else. Like the drink tattooed on her butt, she was the perfect mix of sweet and sour.

Behind her back a beaming smile broke out over my face.

I was already screwed before we even went in the bedroom.

CHAPTER
Twelve

Mila

April 4th, 2018 - Wednesday

Falling into bed with Louis was becoming a habit. I should have told him where to go and just let myself be categorized as mentally incompetent, but my family would use it against me if they got hold of that information so no way was that happening. After we'd spent a couple of hours in bed, I packed some belongings as I reluctantly agreed I may as well try to understand Louis' career as a YouTuber, and he needed to be around his friends. Apparently he was getting a hard time from them, and it wasn't as much fun as the 'hard' time I was getting off him.

I called Jenny to update her about everything. She was busy with work and just told me she was jealous of all the sex I was getting and that she'd be in touch when she got a minute.

"Hey, Mila." Jonno said when I was introduced to them all again.

"Hey, boys." I acknowledged them. "So, I took a couple of days vacation to show you Vegas properly before you go home. Are you ready to experience Vegas at its finest?"

"Ah, man. You mean the helicopter ride don't you?" Jonno's shoulders slumped.

"Hell, no. I think you need to get to know me a little better. Now follow me."

I took them to TopGolf where they were pleasantly surprised by being able to play, eat, drink, and listen to the live bands. Then Wednesday night I told them I was taking them to see Cirque de Soleil. I saw them pull faces, but I put my finger to my lips and said "Trust Me". The show was called Zumanity and a mix between Cabaret and Burlesque. After the show started the guys never took their eyes off the stage, although Louis' hands kept trying to wander, especially when two women were writhing around in a large fishbowl together.

"Holy fuck, that was hot. I need to get laid now." Jonno said, and I laughed.

"That, I'm not helping with."

Me and Louis separated from the rest of them at that point and we returned to his hotel room.

After satisfying Louis's urges following the show we chatted. "Your friends seem good people."

"Yeah, they're great guys."

"Cam seems quiet."

Louis scrubbed a hand through his hair. "Something's going on with him. Cam's not usually this quiet. He doesn't seem himself. He was okay when we first got here. I dunno..." He trailed off.

I hesitated a moment. "Is it because of me?"

Louis' forehead creased as he thought. "I guess you changed the dynamic, but it could be something else. We're guys, we don't talk about stuff. I'll ask him when we get home."

"Well, your friends come first, Louis. So I can make my exit if needed."

He pulled me back toward him. "You're going nowhere."

April 5th, 2018 - Thursday

Thursday, I took the guys to a day party at one of the hotels. It all took place around the pool so they swam, drank, and ate. With the guys it was all about their appetites rather than the usual tourist stuff. Louis recorded events everywhere we went, and I saw his interest in capturing his surroundings. It was like he wanted to show people how to enjoy life more rather than record himself. I got more of an understanding of what he was about.

Thursday night, all I did was smirk when the guys asked me where we were going. As we reached Fremont Street, the light show was in full flow. We stopped and watched the last minute of it.

"That's cool. Shame we weren't here a bit earlier." Jonno said. "Look at those crazy people up there." He pointed to the people on wires above us.

I smiled. "Totally crazy."

Then I took them to the Slotzilla to do exactly that.

"What the fuck is this?" Max asked. "You want me to go up there?"

"You scared, Max boy?" I giggled. "We're all going to be harnessed up and when the next light show starts, we're ziplining the whole way down."

"We're doing what now?" Cam asked. It was one of the rare times he actually spoke directly to me.

"Get your cameras safely secured guys, because

you're traveling the whole way down the street, high in the air next to the lights."

It was a blast. I loved anything that made my adrenaline rise. I was a total adrenaline junkie. The evening made me realize that since my ex had left I'd been hiding away. Meeting Louis had forced me to live life again.

As I waited for the rest of them to finish, my heart sank as I thought that in just over twenty-four hours time, Louis would be heading back to the UK and this would all be over.

"Whooooo. That was insane. I loved it. What's next?" Louis asked.

"Go-karting. You're all going to get beaten by a girl. The shame."

They didn't. They were too competitive for that and all played dirty to force me off the track, but I didn't care. I was having a good time participating and enjoying watching them enjoying themselves. Part of me wished I'd taken Friday off too, but then again, I guessed there was no point postponing the inevitable—that it was all about to end.

I spent another night in Louis' arms.

April 6th, 2018 - Friday

The next morning I got up early. Louis was still sleeping, and I took care not to disturb him before heading home to shower and change before coming back to the strip and going to work.

"I cannot believe you got married drunk. After all you said about the customers who do that." Summer shook her head at me.

"I know. What can I say? The alcohol here must have love potions in it. I now stand corrected."

"So what are you going to do?" She pushed her ash-blonde hair off her face.

"Well an annulment won't work, so I guess get divorced." I broke off to ask a customer what they wanted to drink.

"You don't seem very happy about that?"

I held a finger up and finished serving my customer.

"I'm not." I confessed. "Really, I should be. I should be grateful that the whole mistake will get sorted out eventually, but I just feel sad. I like Louis. A lot. If he lived here, maybe we could have dated? But he doesn't, so I'm gonna pull up my big girl panties and get on with my life. He has shown me that I've been hiding away and not living it, so that's something."

As I got to the end of my shift, I checked my cell again. Louis had kept texting throughout my shift saying I had to come to his as soon as I finished that he was missing me. He didn't mention the elephant in that hotel room. That he would be packing to go home.

I left the bar and then heard my name called as I began to walk down the lobby.

I turned to see Billy, my ex... and my parent's PR person.

Oh, did you think he'd left me for another woman? Oh no. My parents took care of him. He could work for them or have his life ruined. They were good like that. Why did you think I hadn't wanted anything more to do with any of them?

"Billy. What are you doing here?" I put a hand on my hip.

"We need to talk."

"No we really don't. I have nothing to say to you at all. Nothing." I began to walk away.

"You really fucked up this time." His voice was mocking in tone.

I turned back around. "No, I didn't actually.

Louis is the best thing that's happened to me in a long time."

"Your parents want you to get the annulment quietly, and for you to come home and take your place as the rightful heiress to the business. It's time you embraced your responsibilities."

"And if I don't?"

"I'm being paid an exorbitant amount of money to bring you home through any means necessary and I don't intend to fail, so I'll just release the video of you giving me head to the press if you don't go back."

"Fuck you." I spat out. "I already paid you a shit ton of money to destroy that. You said you'd got rid of it and I had the only copy."

"Well, you should know by now that I'm a liar who will get on by any means necessary."

"And you should know I'm a YouTuber who videos absolutely everything and your whole blackmail/extortion threat is here on my phone." Louis barreled up to Josh, getting up in his business. "Now here's what's going to happen. You are going to fuck right back off to the sewer you crawled out of and if you come near Mila again, I'm taking this to the police. Get rid of that video if you know what's good for you."

Billy sighed. "Be cool, dude. I didn't really still

have it. I was bluffing. Now there's no need for any drama." He turned to me. "I'll tell your parents you're a complete waste of space and a lost cause. I have another idea of something they can do anyway."

He walked off.

"Are you okay?" Louis walked over to my side.

My eyes filled with tears. "No. I'm not. I'm really not. Thank you for what you did but right now I just want to be alone."

"Mila. I go home tomorrow. We need to talk."

I shook my head. "There's nothing more to say. Billy showing up made me realize that I make rash, stupid decisions when it comes to men and I'm better off on my own."

"You don't mean that. Mila I-"

I held my hand up.

"Louis, I know you're going home tomorrow but I need time. I'm sorry, but I'm going home—alone. Thank you for what you did though. You saved me." I just wanted my safe place, my apartment, so I walked away from him.

CHAPTER
Thirteen

Louis

Friday 6 April 2018

It was our last day together before my flight home and I couldn't wait for Mila to come to me. I decided to go meet her. Because I'd realised something.

I didn't want to go home if she wasn't coming with me.

I didn't want us to end.

When I heard that douche bag threaten her, I'd had to hold my fists by my sides so I didn't end up in a cell instead of spending these last hours with her. It was time for me to tell her how I felt.

But she refused when I said I needed to talk to her. I was desperate to get the words out but as I said,

"Mila, I-" she interrupted me. And then she left me standing there.

The words 'I love you' on the end of my tongue.

I appreciated she needed her space. But I had hours remaining before I had to get on that plane. It was time to commandeer the troops. Because I needed my wife back.

"The dickhead did what?" Cam's face was masked with fury. It surprised me given his previous attitude.

"I thought you might be happy. You didn't seem such a Mila fan." I told him, raising the question I'd had all week.

Cam sighed. "It was all so fast, and us guys had been with you from the off. I thought for a while you were so hell bent on your subscriber numbers that you were forgetting your mates had been on this crazy ride with you."

I leaned over and knuckled the top of his head. "Never, mate. You're stuck with me and my crazy for life."

"Yeah, I know that, and I also realised life moves on. We do need to grow up. I watched with Mila, and well, I saw how you two are with each other and I want that. I've been single for a long time, since me and Steph broke up, and it's time. Time for me to get back on the horse."

"Dude. I love you, man." I held out a bro fist.

He returned the bro fist and laughed at me. "Yeah, how about saving that love for the missus? So what's the plan then? We need to go get your girl."

CHAPTER
Fourteen

Mila

Being alone wasn't happening because Max had called Jenny, who called me. She refused my pleas of wallowing in self-pity and showed up on my doorstep armed with wine, and Ben & Jerry's.

"Come in." I told her, walking back through to my living room and flopping back onto the couch.

Dressed in my pjs, I threw my comforter I'd dragged to the couch over myself and huddled down.

Jenny walked back in with the Ben & Jerry's and a spoon. I eyed it. Cookie Dough. Yup I was gonna eat that and wallow some more.

I reached over for it and tucked in.

"So, spill. Billy turned up, yeah?"

I licked the back of the spoon. "Do I actually

have to tell you everything or do you already know it all?"

She shrugged. "I want to hear it from you."

"But you're interrupting valuable ice-cream time."

"You're interrupting your life, which is worse."

I put the ice cream on the table.

"Billy turned up and threatened to show a video of me giving him a blow job if I didn't go back home and become the dutiful daughter again. Now thankfully Louis heard and recorded it all because, Jenny, I do not know what I could have done if he hadn't."

I broke down into tears. It was what I needed. To let everything out. I sobbed so hard I felt I'd be sick, but no way was I revisiting epic Ben & Jerry's so I sat up and tried to compose myself. Jenny had wrapped me in a massive hug and held me while I cried.

"Mila. I can't even begin to imagine how it feels to have parents like yours."

"I don't even know what I did wrong. Growing up, I was everything they ever wanted, but it was never enough. They always wanted more from me. In the end I couldn't take it anymore and I ran away. But I wanted to prove them wrong. To go off with someone they'd see as not good enough and settle down and show them they were wrong. Not only did that backfire they hired him for fuck's sake!"

"They aren't normal, Mila."

"Their whole relationship is a sham. They don't love each other. They've both had numerous affairs, but they manage to pay everyone off who would say anything. Their whole relationship is branding. It's all for show. I hate them. I hate that they couldn't be the parents I needed them to be."

I started crying again.

Jenny picked up the ice cream and walked out of the room. I heard the freezer door shut and then glasses clunking and she came back with wine glasses, the rest of the bottle, and some tissues hanging out of her pants pocket.

I drank my wine while Jenny consoled me about the fact my parents were utter shits.

After about thirty minutes Jenny fixed her gaze on mine. "Now. I want you to tell me about Louis."

I sniffed. "What about him?"

"I want to know how you really feel about him, and about the fact that he's leaving tomorrow."

I sighed. "It doesn't really matter how I feel does it? Tomorrow he'll be gone."

"Well, he will if that's your attitude. Frankly, I thought you had more balls than that."

I sat up. "What do you mean?"

"I'll ask you again. How do you really feel about Louis?"

I chewed on my lip. "This is going to sound insane."

"I don't care, just tell me."

"Jenny... I actually think I love him."

And it was the truth. There was just something about the man that had hit me the first time I'd ever set eyes on him. Just this huge connection like life had sent me the person I was destined to be with.

"And so now you're going to give up on the person you feel you love and let him fly back home?"

I shrugged.

Jenny reached over and filled up my glass.

"Bitch, you trying to get me drunk?"

"Hella, yeah. Drunk Mila makes better decisions. Now get that down you, get dressed, and let's go."

"Go where?"

"To meet your husband and stop you from ruining your life."

We pulled up to The Strip in a cab and I followed Jenny to a boutique. "Jenny. What are we doing here? I thought we were meeting the guys?"

"You are." Louis walked in dressed in a dark suit,

a white shirt, and gray tie. Oh my God, I just wanted to rip every stitch of clothing from his body there and then and get him to use that tie on my wrists.

"What's going on?" I asked.

Jenny melted away into the background and Louis took my hand in his.

"Mila. We met not even a week ago and I know it's totally crazy but I feel like our wedding was the best rash, insane decision I ever made. But it annoys me that you don't remember it. I don't want you to let me go home tomorrow with only a plan of a future divorce."

He dropped to a bended knee.

Holy crap!

"Mila Williams. I love you. I know it's stupid and we only just met, but I do. We have the rest of our lives to get to know each other. I can move to Vegas, or you can come to the UK. Fuck, we can move to Timbuktu if you want. But please, marry me again. Marry me relatively sober so you can remember it this time."

"And this boutique hires out wedding dresses." Jenny shouted.

My heart skipped a beat. "Yes! Yes, Louis Clayton. I will marry you. In the most outrageous wedding possible that you can put together in the short time we have, and I don't care where we live either. We'll sort all that later. What matters is I feel the same. I love you too."

He picked me up and whisked me around.

"Go get your dress and we'll see you at the Chapel."

This time we were married by a dwarf 'Alan' from the hangover, complete with monkey. It was appropriate given the circumstances of our first wedding. But yes, this time I did actually remember it and lo and behold... Louis didn't record it.

Yes, you could only have it filmed by the chapel themselves, but we agreed that this ceremony was private. I'd found a fantastic tight short white dress that molded to my figure and had teamed it with a small tiara. Accepting I wasn't a traditional girl, it was time for me to embrace exactly who I really was.

"I now pronounce you husband and wife... again."

We went back to Louis' hotel room at the MGM grand where he carried me over the threshold. I giggled as he headed straight for the bed where he carefully deposited me on the comforter.

"I'd love to tear your clothes off right now but unfortunately they have to back to the shop tomorrow." Louis said.

"Yeah, it's a pity." I replied, but we could take each other's clothes off reaaallly slllooowwwwllly.

And we did. With nibbles, caresses, bites, licks, and sucks.

Finally naked, Louis sank himself inside me while his fingers strummed my clit. I slipped my hand between us and put a finger either side of his dick and moved them up and down the base of his cock with a slight pressure.

"You're killing me here Mrs Clayton." He groaned.

"Oh I hope not. I need you to stay alive so you can continue to satisfy me for hours yet."

"Okay, I'll try my best to survive." He said, and then he hardened his thrusts and quickened his strumming until I could barely remember my own name.

April 7th, 2018 - Saturday

When I woke the next morning I turned to my side to see my new husband packing his things. The smile I'd woken up with slipped from my face as I remembered he was leaving. He came over to me, knelt at the side of the bed and stroked a hand down my face. "I'm only going home to sort a few things out, Mila. Then I'll be back. Here before you know it."

"I know, but I'm gonna miss the shit out of you."

He laughed, that big hearty laugh of his. "Which is really funny when you think this time last week we didn't even know each other existed."

"So you're really gonna come live here for a while?"

"Yeah if the laws allow it. Plus there's my mother to get past. I didn't invite her to my first wedding. She's gonna have my balls for not being at the second."

"Oh, let's just keep getting married then. I like marrying you." I said leaning over to kiss him.

Epilogue

Mila

It took a year of legal wrangling with only occasional visits to each other before Louis' visa was approved. He moved into my apartment. I'd like to say it was all plain sailing but it wasn't. Some times were hard, we had huge arguments. But neither of us had lived with anyone before and we realized we were adjusting to our new lives together. Louis did change his channel. His vlogs of the different aspects of Vegas had gone down really well and he found himself with multiple offers from Vegas businesses to showcase their venues and events, and then we had our own reality channel. I was very careful about what we showed. I'd gotten used to my every move being recorded but there were still times when I said no. Like when we'd gotten married a third time in the UK so his family could attend. (By the way I loved Louis' mother).

But today I walked in with my own phone, recording Louis' face as he sat down on our second wedding anniversary to a home cooked breakfast.

"Hey, hubby. Happy anniversary."

"Hey, wife." He looked at the silver server in front of him. "This is very elaborate for a slice of toast."

"I cooked you a full English, you jerk." I said. "Okay, now you can eat."

He lifted off the lid to find there was no food. Instead there was a pregnancy test stick.

Louis went pale.

"Mila. Are you saying that...?"

I grinned. "You're gonna be a dad. Happy anniversary, baby."

"Oh my God, that's amazing. That's so frikking amazing. He jumped up and down and picked up the stick to look at it.

Then he threw it down and stared at his hand.

"You peed on that, didn't you?"

"That's usually how those work."

"Ah well, I always wanted to move onto golden showers. It's kind of a step towards it."

"Louis. For God's sake." I said as I put down the phone because I was then lifted off my feet.

"That is totally not going on the channel now."

"Yeah it is."

"No, it's not."

"So, in tribute to your ass tattoo I think Martin for a boy and Martina for a girl."

"Our child is not being named after an ass tattoo."

But my protests were drowned out as Louis' mouth crushed mine.

THE END

ALL ABOUT ANGEL

All About Angel

I like writing short sexy stories that get readers hot under the collar while also entertaining and hopefully making the reader laugh.

Keep in contact with me here at

www.facebook.com/angeldevlinauthor

THE COCKTAIL GIRLS

It's time to get drunk on love!
The Cocktail Girls is a shared world between 14 of
your favorite romance authors!

Each novella is a stand-alone story set in the city
of sin.

Start your summer off right: beginning May 31st, a
title or two will release daily.

Grab your kindle, a cocktail, and get ready to meet
our new swoon-worthy alphas!

Cheers!

His Sloe Screw by Alexandria Hunt

His Old Fashioned by Frankie Love

His Redheaded Slut by Vivian Ward

His Whiskey Sour by Kim Loraine

His Hurricane by Alexis Adaire

His Perfect Martini by Angel Devlin

His Mimosa by Jamie Schlosser

His Manhattan by Tracy Lorraine

His Long Island Iced Tea by Roxy Sinclaire

His Gin and Juice by Alexx Andria

His Irish Coffee by Jessica Lake

His Blushing Bride by Emilia Beaumont

His Champagne by Dori Lavelle

His Vegas Bomb by Derek Masters

Find your favourite authors in one place!

www.subscribepage.com/bookhangoverlounge

Join us in the Book Hangover Lounge for giveaways and goodies ... and the perfect place to recover from a long night with your latest book boyfriend!

Printed in Great Britain
by Amazon